We played in the streets!
We played hopscotch and jacks and double Dutch.
And boys hit pink rubber balls with broomsticks and
raced around on go-carts made of orange crates or old
baby carriages.

High up on the roofs, my best friend's brother waved
clouds of pet pigeons this way and that with a flag made
of rags.

BeBop-a-do-Walk!

by Sheila Hamanaka

SIMON & SCHUSTER BOOKS FOR YOUNG READERS

To "Ham" Hamanaka,
one cool daddy

SIMON & SCHUSTER BOOKS FOR YOUNG READERS
An Imprint of Simon & Schuster Children's Publishing Division.
1230 Avenue of the Americas, New York, NY 10020.
Copyright © 1995 by Sheila Hamanaka. All rights reserved,
including the right of reproduction in whole or in part in any form.
SIMON & SCHUSTER BOOKS FOR YOUNG READERS is a trademark of
Simon & Schuster. Designed by Christy Hale. The text of this book
is set in Impress. The illustrations were rendered in acrylic.
Manufactured in Hong Kong by South China Printing Company
(1988) Ltd. 10 9 8 7 6 5 4 3 2 1

Library of Congress Cataloging-in-Publication Data
Hamanaka, Sheila. Bebop-a-do-walk! / by Sheila Hamanaka. —
1st ed. p. cm. Summary: On a walk to Central Park a Japanese-
American child's father folds paper hats and boats to sail on the
pond and then paper cranes to fly on their bus ride home.
ISBN: 0-689-80288-9 [Walking—Fiction. 2. New York
(N.Y.)—Fiction. 3. Oragami—Fiction. 4. Japanese Americans—
Fiction.] Title. PZ7.H169Lo 1995 [E]—dc20
94-14235

At night in vacant lots, neighbors roasted potatoes in big bonfires, and the sparks floated up to the stars.

But best thing of all was the longest walk.

My father liked to take long walks by himself, and one day my best friend, Martha, and I were bored and begged him to take us along.

"Okay, Emi. Okay, Martha," he said, "but it's going to be a long one. I'm going to see Carlos and then I'm going

to see Bob and then I'm going to see Norman and then
I'm going to the park to do some sketching. And I'm not
taking the bus."

A long walk! We had to get ready! Martha made jelly
sandwiches, and I packed split peas for the pigeons.

We ran downstairs and took one last look at our
building. Our neighbors waved from their windows. Mr.
Murillo waved from the third floor and Mrs. Schwartz
waved from the second and Linda Chin and her dog,
Pinky, looked down from the fire escape above us.
"We're going for a walk!" Martha shouted.

"The longest walk!" I said. "All the way to Central
Park! Good-bye!"

"Bye-bye," said Mr. Murillo.

"Adios," called Mrs. Schwartz.

Pinky barked, and Linda looked jealous and frowned.

"That's too far," she warned. "You're going to get tired."

We were off! Past the grumpy knish man, past Louie in the pickle store, past Patty in the delicatessen, where the spicy smell of hot pastrami on rye (with mustard, please) followed us down the street . . . right into Tom's candy store.

"We're going on a long walk," Martha told Tom.

"A really long walk," I added. "All the way to Central Park! We need two chocolate-covered cherries and a candy necklace, please."

As we ran out the door, we heard Tom calling, "Wait! Here's a present for the squirrels." And he threw us a bag of peanuts.

"Thanks, Mr. Tom!"

We stopped for a second to leave our nose prints on the window of the bakery with its trays of cannoli, chocolate éclairs, cream puffs, and assorted dreamy cookies. We waved good-bye to the tiny bride and groom peering down at us from the top of a giant wedding cake, and we were off again.

My father caught up with us and made us stop at
the corner. Honking cars, buses, and taxis whizzed by,
as more and more people gathered to wait for the
light. Then the light flashed green, and Martha and I
led the charge across the street.

We walked and walked, heading north to Washington
Square Park. A crowd was gathering around the fountain
to listen to a man beating bongo drums.

"Carlos!" my father yelled. Carlos stopped drumming and waved.

We told him we were on a very long walk all the way to Central Park, and he said, "Groovy! Don't forget to look for King Kong when you get to the Empire State Building."

And we were off again, farther north through Union
Square, past the Flatiron Building, and on to the
Empire State Building, where Martha swore you could
see King Kong, but only if you looked out of the corner
of your eye and hopped on one foot.

My father said, "Step lively, ladies! I've got to meet
Bob on Fifty-second Street and give him back his book.
It's a swinging street."

And it was! Bob had a monkey named Dizzy, and
Dizzy and Martha and I swung around every lamppost
on the block.

Bob said, "Girls, this used to be the hottest street in
town! Every night jazz clubs were hoppin', musicians
were be-boppin'. Your Dad and I listened to Bird and Diz
and Monk . . . BE-bop-a-DO-op-oolya'CU, oolya'CU—
Be-bop-she-BAM!" Then Bob took out his trumpet and
played for us. We swung around and around until we
could imagine all the people and lights!

By now we were close to the Museum of Modern Art, where my father had to meet Norman. Inside, Martha and I giggled at the largest painting we'd ever seen. "I'd get in trouble if I threw paint around like that!" Martha said.

We were pretty tired, so we decided to sit down on
the floor. Out of the corner of our eyes, we saw a guard
who looked as big as a giant balloon sneaking up on us.
He tiptoed closer and closer. But instead of yelling, he
gave us each a red-and-white-striped peppermint. Yum!

We didn't think we could walk any farther, but before we knew it, we were in Central Park. The sun winked at us through the trees, and the ground was a scrunchy carpet covered with grass and dandelions. We dropped split peas and peanuts, and a parade of pigeons and squirrels followed us all the way to the carousel.

The carousel!

"Can we go for a ride?" we begged. My father nodded and bought tickets, and we jumped on. The music started, and the park began to spin around and around, and the horses ran so fast we had to hold on tight.

And can you believe we walked some more?
   Yes, we walked until we reached a pond. My father
sat down and took out his sketch pad. There were people
all around, and there were little boats floating in the pond.

I saw a boy walking toward us. He was with a woman who was dressed like a nurse. That boy was carrying the most beautiful toy sailboat I had ever seen.

"Can we see your boat?" I asked.

"No," he said.

He put it in the water and gave it a little push. The wind
made the sails billow, and the boat glided away in a
graceful arc. Martha and I stood by and watched.

"Emi, I've got a boat for you," my father called out.
"And one for you, too, Martha." I thought he was making
a joke. He hadn't brought anything with him but his old
sketch pad. But suddenly he tore out a page and began
folding. He folded one boat! And then another!

"And here are two hats for the two admirals!" He folded the hats from an old newspaper. We raced to the pond and launched our boats.

Soon other kids ran over, and my father made boats
and hats for them, too.

The pond was filled with a paper fleet!

Finally the boy with the sailboat walked up and
said, "Can I have one, too?"

I wanted my father to say no, but instead he
smiled at the boy and said, "Surely."

I was mad, but it turned out okay because after
that the boy let Martha and me sail his boat. We even
gave him half a jelly sandwich, and the woman dressed

like a nurse gave us candied chestnuts wrapped in
pretty foil paper.

    Before we knew it, the sky had begun to turn
orange at the edges and it was time to go. I
remembered that we had to walk home and suddenly
I felt really tired. Martha and I walked slowly behind
my father until we got to the edge of the park.

"Can we take a bus, Daddy?"

I expected him to say no, but instead he smiled at me and said, "Surely."

When the bus came, the three of us hopped on and my father dropped his last fifteen cents in the box.

The bus was warm and humming and bumping
along, and we almost fell asleep. But then my father
took out his old sketch pad and began folding paper
cranes for everyone on the bus. No one even noticed
the city with its twinkling lights as our bus full of
people and cranes flew down the street.

The
End